This Book
Has Been Donated
In Honor of
_Peyton_____ 's

7th Birthday

Understanding
Volcanoes and
Earthquakes

Jen Green

PowerKiDS
press.
New York

Published in 2008 by The Rosen Publishing Group, Inc.
29 East 21st Street, New York, NY 10010

First Edition

Picture credits:
Cover Digital Vision, 1 Digital Vision, 4 iStockphoto.com, 5 Digital Vision, 6 Dreamstime.com/Matthew Eggington, 7 Science Photo Library/Gary Hincks, 8 Dreamstime.com/Paul Prescott, 9 Alamy/Arctic Images, 10 Digital Vision, 11 Digital Vision, 12 Corbis/Ralph White, 13 NASA,14 Dreamstime.com/Adam Booth, 15 Dreamstime.com/Patrick Ryan, 16 Corbis/Roger Ressmeyer, 17 Corbis/Lloyd Cluff, 18 iStockphoto.com, 19 Getty Images/STF/AFP, 20 Getty Images/Carsten Peter/National Geographic, 21 Dreamstime.com

Produced by Tall Tree Ltd.
Editor: Jon Richards
Designer: Ben Ruocco
Consultant: John Williams

Library of Congress Cataloging-in-Publication Data

Green, Jen.
  Understanding volcanoes and earthquakes / Jen Green. — 1st ed.
      p. cm. — (Our Earth)
  Includes index.
  ISBN-13: 978-1-4042-4276-0 (library binding)
  1. Volcanoes—Juvenile literature. 2. Earthquakes—Juvenile literature. I. Title.
  QE521.3.G734 2008
  551.21—dc22
                                          2007032600

Manufactured in China

Contents

Volcanoes and earthquakes

Volcanoes and earthquakes are powerful natural forces. Red-hot rock, ash, and **steam** shoot out of a volcano. Earthquakes shake the ground and damage buildings.

⬇ These buildings were damaged by a powerful earthquake.

Volcanoes and earthquakes are caused by powerful forces deep inside the Earth.

⬇ Red-hot rock called **lava** shoots out from a volcano.

What is the Earth?

The Earth is the planet we live on. It has three main layers: the hard **crust**, a hot layer called the **mantle**, and the **core** in the middle. The rocks on the surface are hard. The rocks inside glow red-hot, and flow like liquid.

⊗ At its thickest, the Earth's crust is only 60 miles (100 km) deep.

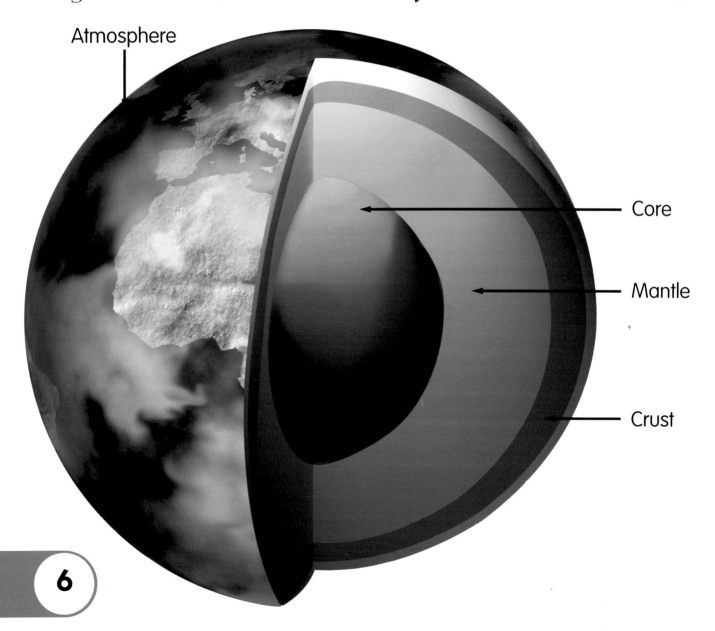

Atmosphere

Core

Mantle

Crust

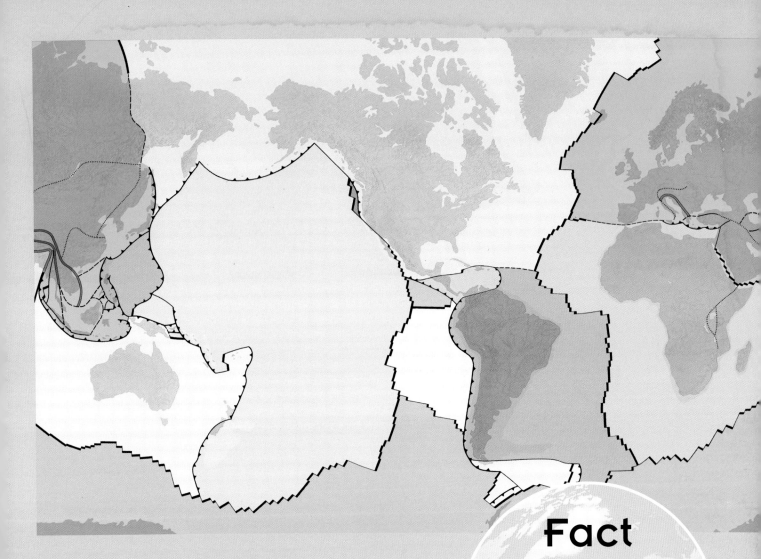

⬥ Earth's crust is made up of huge pieces that fit together like a jigsaw puzzle.

Fact

Millions of years ago, all of the Earth's islands were joined in one enormous island called Pangaea.

Earth's outer layer is called the crust. It is cracked into huge pieces called **plates**. They float like rafts on the hot, **molten** rocks below. The Earth's seas and land sit on top of these plates.

The moving crust

The giant plates that make up the crust are not fixed in one place. Movements in the red-hot layer below send them drifting across the Earth's surface.

Where plates bump together, the rocks crumple upward to form mountains.

⬀ The island of Surtsey near Iceland was created when lava poured out of a crack formed by two plates moving apart.

Fact

Earth's plates drift about 1 inch (2.5 cm) a year. Your fingernails grow at the same speed.

Drifting plates may slowly scrape past each other, separate, or bump into each other. This can make mountains rise, earthquakes strike, and volcanoes **erupt**.

Volcanic eruptions

Volcanoes are holes in the crust where lava, steam, and gas escape. This is called an eruption. The lava, steam, and gas pour out of an opening called a **crater**.

❯❯ Some volcanoes throw out ash and rocks high into the air.

As lava flows out of the volcano, it cools and becomes hard rock. Over time, this rock builds up to form a high mountain.

Fact

In 1883, Krakatau volcano in Indonesia exploded. The bang was heard 2,800 miles (4,500 km) away!

❯ The temperature of lava can be 2,200°F (1,200°C).

Undersea volcanoes

Many volcanoes lie underwater on the seabed. They form where the Earth's plates drift apart. This leaves a crack, out of which lava flows.

⬇ **Black smokers** are underwater volcanoes that throw out clouds of black, boiling water.

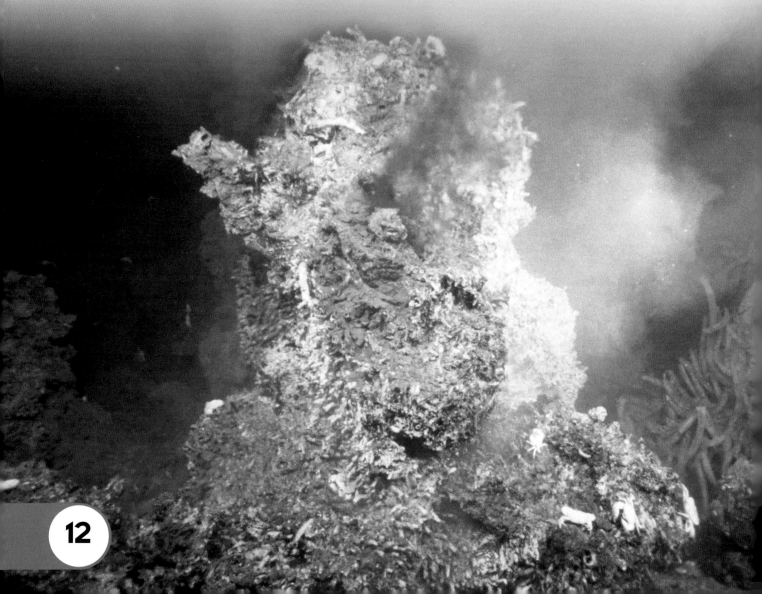

Some undersea volcanoes erupt for a long time. The mound of lava slowly builds up and may rise above the sea to make a new island. The islands of Hawaii in the Pacific are a chain of volcanoes.

Fact

A line of undersea volcanoes called the Mid-Atlantic Ridge is the world's longest mountain chain.

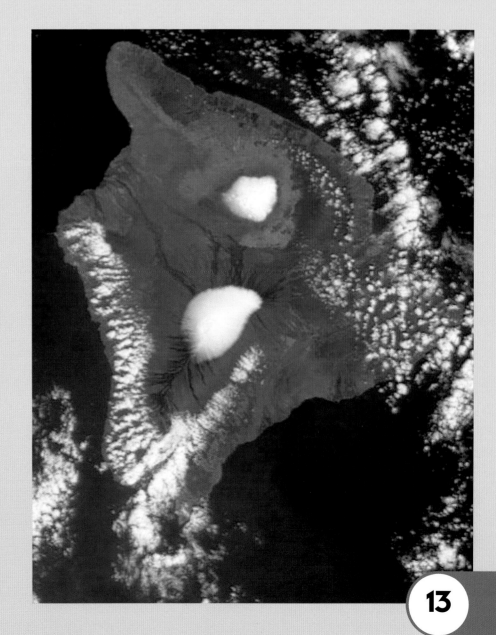

❯❯ The island of Hawaii is home to a volcano called Mauna Loa, which is the largest volcano on Earth.

13

Geysers and hot springs

Hot springs are sometimes found near volcanoes. Water under the ground is heated by the **volcanic** rocks and it gushes to the surface. Sometimes, soil mixed with hot springs forms pools of smelly, bubbling mud.

▶▶ Hot gases from underground rise to the surface, causing the mud to bubble.

Geysers are hot springs that shoot jets of steam and boiling water into the air. In Iceland, people use hot springs to heat houses and produce electricity.

Fact

Steamboat Geyser in Yellowstone National Park shoots a jet of water up to 380 ft. (115 m) high.

❯❯ Old Faithful Geyser in California spouts every 60 to 70 minutes.

Shaking the Earth

Earthquakes occur in areas where the plates move against each other. However, the plates do not move smoothly. They can move into position with a sudden jolt, causing the ground to shake violently.

❯❯ In 1989, an earthquake in San Francisco wrecked many buildings.

Small earthquakes make light bulbs swing and crockery rattle. Bigger ones can shatter windows. The worst earthquakes crack the ground and damage buildings and bridges.

The San Andreas **fault** in California is where two of the Earth's plates are rubbing past each other.

Tsunamis and landslides

When earthquakes or eruptions shake the seabed, they can cause huge waves called **tsunamis**. The waves spread out like giant ripples. When they reach shallow water, they form enormous waves.

This town in Indonesia was destroyed by the Asian tsunami that hit on December 26, 2004.

Fact

Tsunamis can travel 590 mph (950 km/h) and reach 100 ft. (30 m) high along the coast.

On land, earthquakes can cause rocks and mud to slip down a mountain. This is called a **landslide** and it will damage anything in its path.

⬆ The town of Armero in Colombia was destroyed by a landslide in 1985.

Volcano and earthquake safety

Scientists study volcanoes and areas at risk of earthquakes. They look for signs that a volcano might erupt or that an earthquake may occur.

This scientist is studying a volcano by collecting samples of lava.

Fact

In 1975, everyone was told to leave Haicheng in China after an earthquake warning. Two hours later, the earthquake struck!

In 2002, the volcano of Mount Nyiragongo in the Democratic Republic of Congo erupted. People were moved away and had to live in temporary housing.

If scientists believe a disaster will strike, they can raise the alarm and people can leave the area quickly. This can save thousands of lives. However, earthquakes and eruptions still strike without giving any warning at all.

Activities

Make your own volcano

Watch as the red, bubbling "lava" flows out of the crater of your own erupting volcano.

WHAT YOU NEED

- **Empty bottle**
- **Large dish**
- **Baking soda**
- **Vinegar**
- **Red food coloring**
- **Dish detergent**
- **Jug and spoon**

1. Place an empty bottle in the middle of the large dish. Use the spoon to fill the bottom of the bottle with baking soda.

2. Mix the vinegar with a few drops of the food coloring and two drops of dish detergent.

3. Pour the mixture into the bottle and watch the volcano erupt.

The vinegar and the baking soda mix to form a bubbling liquid.

Build a simple tilt machine

The ground around a volcano moves as liquid rock is forced into the volcano just before it erupts. A tilt machine measures the angle of these movements.

WHAT YOU NEED

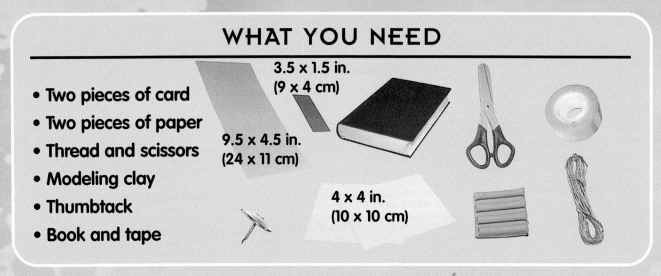

- Two pieces of card
- Two pieces of paper
- Thread and scissors
- Modeling clay
- Thumbtack
- Book and tape

3.5 x 1.5 in. (9 x 4 cm)

9.5 x 4.5 in. (24 x 11 cm)

4 x 4 in. (10 x 10 cm)

1. Fold the large piece of card. Cut the smaller piece of card diagonally, and tape one of the pieces inside the fold of the large piece to support it.

2. Mark a scale on the paper by drawing lines as shown. Tape this to the card.

3. Put a piece of modeling clay on one end of the thread. Use the thumbtack to fasten the other end to the scale.

4. Put the tilt meter on the book. Moving the book copies the ground movements during an eruption. Watch as the thread moves with the book, and record the angle of the tilt.

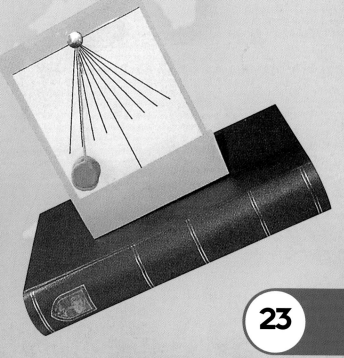

23

Glossary

Black smokers Undersea volcanoes that spout dark clouds of hot water.

Core The region at the very center of the Earth.

Crater An opening in the top of a volcano.

Crust The outer layer of the Earth.

Erupt When a volcano comes to life and gives off ash, gas, steam, and lava.

Fault A crack formed by moving rocks.

Geysers Hot springs that spout steam and boiling water high into the air.

Landslide When a mass of mud, rock, and soil slips down a hill or mountain.

Lava Hot, molten rock from deep underground that flows onto the Earth's surface.

Mantle Part of the Earth that lies between the core and the crust.

Molten Something that has melted and is liquid.

Plates Huge, stiff sections of rock that make up the Earth's crust.

Steam Water that has been heated until it forms a gas.

Tsunamis Giant waves that are created when an earthquake or volcanic eruption disturbs the seabed.

Volcanic To do with volcanoes.

Index

Web Sites

Due to the changing nature of Internet links, PowerKids Press has developed an online list of Web sites related to the subject of this book. This site is regularly updated. Please use this link to access this list:
www.powerkidslinks.com/earth/volquake